BAD KITTY
SCHOOL
DAZE

NICK BRUEL

SQUARE
FISH

ROARING BROOK PRESS
New York

For all teachers everywhere

Page 83, *The Battle at Bunker's Hill*, George Edward Perine after John Trumbull, courtesy of Emmet Collection, Miriam and Ira D. Wallach Division of Art, Prints and Photographs, The New York Public Library, Astor, Lenox and Tilden Foundations

SQUARE
FISH

An Imprint of Macmillan
175 Fifth Avenue, New York, NY 10010
mackids.com

BAD KITTY SCHOOL DAZE. Copyright © 2013 by Nick Bruel. All rights reserved. Printed in the United States of America by LSC Communications, Harrisonburg, Virginia.

Square Fish and the Square Fish logo are trademarks of Macmillan and are used by Roaring Brook Press under license from Macmillan.

Square Fish books may be purchased for business or promotional use. For information on bulk purchases, please contact the Macmillan Corporate and Premium Sales Department at (800) 221-7945 x 5442 or by e-mail at specialmarkets@macmillan.com.

Library of Congress Cataloging-in-Publication Data
Bruel, Nick.
Bad Kitty school daze / Nick Bruel.
p. cm.
Summary: "When Kitty's owners have finally had enough of her bad behavior, it's time to ship her off to obedience school"— Provided by publisher.
ISBN 978-1-250-03947-7 (Square Fish paperback)
ISBN 978-1-59643-944-3 (Scholastic edition)
[1. Cats—Fiction. 2. Pets—Training—Fiction. 3. Humorous stories.] I. Title.
PZ7.B82832Bao 2012   [E]—dc23   2012015359

Originally published in the United States by Neal Porter Books/Roaring Brook Press
First Square Fish Edition: 2014
Square Fish logo designed by Filomena Tuosto

15 17 19 20 18 16 14

AR: 3.3 / LEXILE: GN630L

• CONTENTS •

•CHAPTER ONE•
ONE FINE DAY

SNORE

Oh, dear! What happened, Baby? Did you fall down? How did that happen?

The cat did this? Well, I'm not surprised. Tsk, tsk, tsk. The way those two were running and horsing around. But I'm sure it was an accident.

Kitty, it's time for us to have a little talk.

Kitty, I've had enough of your SCREAMING and HISSING and FIGHTING. It's time we did something about your behavior, your nasty temper, and the fact that you never seem to listen.

And that goes for you too, Puppy. That drooling problem of yours started all of this.

That's why I've decided it's time for both of you to go to . . .

SCHOOL.

CHAPTER TWO

THE NEXT FINE DAY

HEY, KITTY! I just got back from the store, and look at all of the super-cool school supplies I bought for you! They all feature your absolute FAVORITE . . .

Love Love Angel Kitten

Love Love Angel Kitten
Backpack

Love
Love
Angel
Kitten
Notebook

Love Love Angel Kitten
Eraser

Love Love
Angel Kitten
Pencils

Love Love
Angel Kitten
Bowling Ball

Pinkish
Pink

Reddish
Pink

Deep Pink

Light Pink

Pink

Love Love
Angel Kitten
Crayons

Love Love Angel Kitten
Calculator

Love Love
Angel
Kitten
Gym Shorts

Love Love
Angel Kitten
Tractor
Tire

Love Love
Angel Kitten
Cinder Block

Love Love
Angel Kitten
Ruler

Whew! That's a lot of
stuff! Oh well . . .
Let's put it all into
your backpack.

Awwww, look at you! All ready for school.

And so is Puppy! Did you pack your bandana, Puppy? I hope so, because you'll need it if you start drooling again.

We better hurry. You guys don't want to be late for the school bus!

HERE IT COMES!

UNCLE MURRAY'S FUN FACTS

WHY DO DOGS CHASE CATS?

Hey, don't blame the dog for this!

Dogs don't just chase cats. They chase lots of things, because that's what dogs like to do most.

Herder dogs like border collies are bred to chase sheep and keep the flock together. Hunting dogs like hounds and dachshunds are bred to chase foxes and rats. Police dogs like German shepherds are trained to chase criminals. And dogs chase all of these things not just because they like to do it, but also because

they're so very, very good at it.

When a dog chases a cat, it's not chasing because it's being mean. It's chasing the cat because of instinct. "Instinct" is that part of an animal's brain that controls how an animal is going to act. Birds can fly because their instinct

MEOW*

*Albert Einstein once said that "Peace cannot be kept by force; it can only be achieved by understanding."

tells them how. Fish can swim because their instinct tells them how. And dogs chase other animals because their instinct tells them it's an important thing to do.

So when a dog sees a strange cat for the first time, his brain tells him that he MUST begin chasing the cat. It doesn't help that dogs are also very territorial, which means that if the cat is anywhere near something the dog thinks he owns, like his bone or his backyard or his house or even YOU, then he will feel compelled to chase that poor cat away.

Cats, by the way, have the same instinct as dogs. Cats are extremely good at chasing other animals, only they chase animals much smaller than they are, like mice and rats. Most dogs are bigger, sometimes MUCH bigger, than cats. So cats do not generally chase dogs.

Dogs, however, do not have the same sense of caution as cats and will often chase things much, much bigger than them. That's why they'll sometimes chase cars.

I like dogs, but they better not chase my school bus!

All right, ya goofy cat, move on to the back of the bus and you can meet some of your new classmates!

28

Bye, Kitty! Bye, Puppy! I'll see you at the end of the day!

All right, you guys! Everybody off the bus and welcome to . . .

Well, pets, my name is Diabla von Gloom. But I want you all to call me Miss Dee. Welcome to my school! School, as you may know, is a place where you go to learn something new. So, I really hope that you all learn something new today.

Let's step into the classroom! And as you all head inside, I want you to understand one thing...

40

41

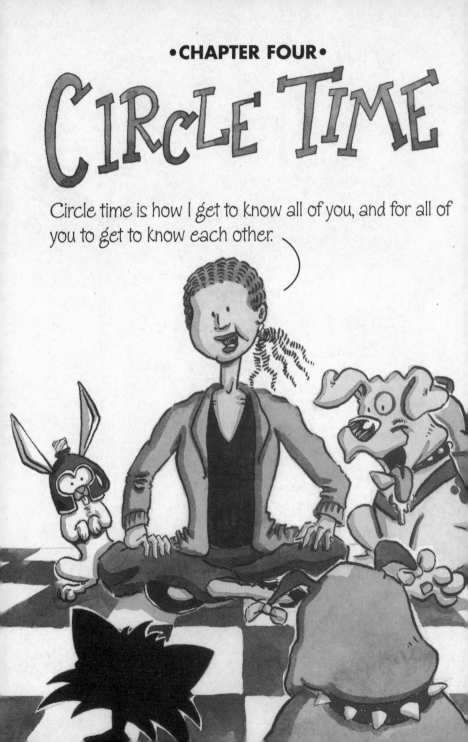

Let's start with you, Petunia. Tell us what's on your mind.

I just hate them! I hate them so much! I hate their eyes! I hate their noses! I hate their goofy-looking whiskers! When I see them, I just want to punch them!

PUNCH!

PUNCH!

PUNCH!

I . . . I . . . just want to bite their heads off and chew their faces like gum! CHEW! CHEW! CHEW! I want to pick them up and throw them all into active volcanos!

I hear ya,
cow sister.

60

61

Stop blaming dogs! This is all the fault of goofy cats!

WHY DO DOGS AND CATS HATE EACH OTHER?

The problem between dogs and cats isn't so much that they hate each other . . . they just don't understand each other. Let's think about how dogs and cats are different from each other.

NOSE- SNIFFS EVERYTHING

TONGUE- LICKS YOU BECAUSE HE LIKES YOU

TAIL- WAGS WHEN HAPPY

Dogs are very social. They live in packs and usually enjoy the company of other dogs. Dogs like to play by wrestling and biting. When a dog first meets you, he likes to sniff you (especially in places where you may not like to be sniffed). When a dog likes you, he expresses it by licking you. When a dog is happy, he wags his tail.

Cats, on the other hand, are not social animals. They lead independent lives and usually do not seek the company of other cats. Except for when they're young, cats do not play with each other and especially not by wrestling or biting. Cats don't sniff things nearly as much as dogs. Cats generally only lick themselves, and then only to clean themselves. And cats only shake their tails when they're feeling nervous or angry.

TAIL—SHAKES WHEN NERVOUS

NOSE—USUALLY ONLY SNIFFS TO SENSE DANGER OR SAFETY

TONGUE—ONLY LICKS HERSELF

Now imagine what happens when a strange dog and cat meet for the first time. The dog runs up to the cat with its tail wagging, expecting to sniff her, lick her, and play with her. But the cat meanwhile sees the dog's running as an attack. She sees the wagging tail as a sign of anger. And the last thing the cat wants is to be sniffed (especially in a place where she doesn't want to be sniffed), licked, and played with. So the cat either runs away or attacks, neither of which the dog expected.

Okay, so maybe the dogs are just kinda sorta partly to blame.

So now the dog has a perception that cats just *aren't* friendly. This isn't going to encourage the dog to be friendly with any cats in the future. And so begins a cycle of misunderstanding that can sometimes lead to a real mess.

CHAPTER FIVE

ARTS + CRAFTS

I want each of you to make me something that depicts what you're thinking about right now!

Hmmm . . . I'm not too sure what to make of this, Petunia. But I do believe we have to find a way for you to make peace with cats.

79

81

85

•CHAPTER SIX•
SHOW + TELL

I want each of you to SHOW me something that's special to you and then TELL me why it's important.

91

95

Okay, Puppy. It's your turn! What are you going to show us?

Wait! Where are you going, little puppy?

Partita in a minor

for Solo Flute

J. S. Bach
BWV 1013

Allemande

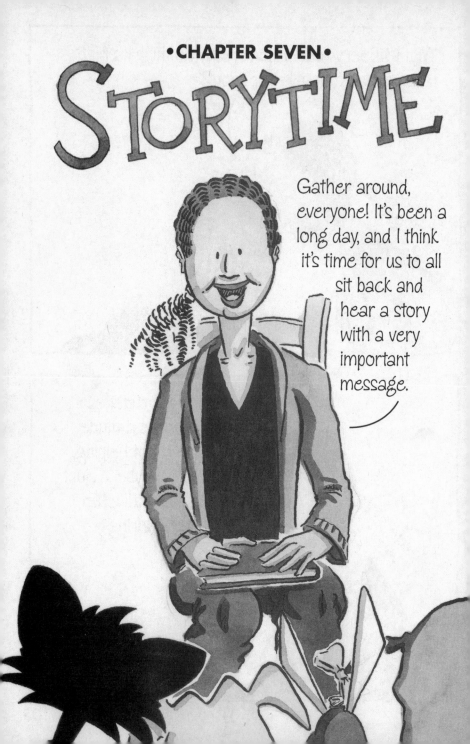

Today's story is "Love Love Angel Kitten and Her Friends on the Farm."

One day, Love Love Angel Kitten decided to go visit the farm.

"Oh, what joy that would be," said Love Love Angel Kitten to herself. "I've never met any farm animals."

"And it's always so very, very fun to make new friends!"

So she stepped into her magic rainbow helicopter made out of candy and . . .

THUD!

But you're not just plain ol' Kitty anymore, are you?
No, now you're . . .

LOVE LOVE
ANGEL KITTY!

HEY, EVERYBODY! Look at Love Love Angel Kitty!

She made dinner for us! She's so very, very KIND!

She bought us all presents! She's so very, very GENEROUS!

She cleaned her own litterbox! She's so very, very HELPFUL!

Love Love Angel Kitty is such a very, very, good, good, GOOD Kitty! Look at how much she loves Baby!

Now look at how much she loves Puppy!

Finally, there is peace in our home. Where once there were screaming temper tantrums, now there are only kisses. Where once there were fights and shrieks and howls, now there are only hugs. Where once there was only mayhem, now there is only love. Sweet, wonderful LOVE.

CHAPTER EIGHT

GRADUATION

Well class, this has been a very full day. But it's time for graduation. Do you remember what I told you school is for? School is where you go to learn something new.

This means that if you can show me that you've learned something new today, then I will give you a diploma to show that you've graduated. And then you can go home happy and proud to know that you will all be better pets.

What a clever puppy! You've learned how to control your drool! Here's your diploma!

PAT PAT

I, DR. LAGOMORPH, HAVE LEARNED TWO THINGS TODAY! TWO, I TELL YOU!

TWO!

FIRST, I HAVE LEARNED THE MYSTIC SECRETS OF TRANSFORMING MY ENEMIES INTO TWENTY-POUND BLOCKS OF GORGONZOLA CHEESE BY USING THIS ANCIENT CRYSTAL I FOUND HERE INSIDE THIS CHAMBER OF LEARNING! I WILL USE IT TO FINALLY DEFEAT THAT DESPICABLE DO-GOODER CAPTAIN FANTASTICAT AND HIS MINISCULE SIDEKICK POWER MOUSE. THEN NOTHING SHALL STAND IN THE WAY OF MY COMPLETE AND TOTAL WORLD DOMINATION!

125

128

OH, HOW WRONG I HAVE BEEN! I HAVE WASTED SO MUCH TIME HATING CATS WHEN I SHOULD HAVE BEEN LOVING THEM AS I DO MY NEW BEST FRIEND!

OOF

FROM THIS MOMENT ON, I SHALL DEDICATE MY LIFE NOT TO CHASING OR BITING OR CHEWING BUT TO LOVING THESE KINDEST AND GENTLEST OF ALL THE EARTH'S CREATURES. NEVER AGAIN WILL I SPEAK ILL OF YOU BEAUTIFUL BEASTS. THIS I VOW!

133

Well, that's too bad.

I'm sorry that you say you didn't learn anything and that you won't graduate today.

But I learned something about you today, Kitty.

Do you want to know what it is?

I watched you help your
puppy friend with his
drooling problem.

I watched you be the first
to support the little bunny
with your applause.

I watched you give Petunia
your painting and make
a new friend.

Do you want to know
what I learned about
you today, Kitty?

I learned that you're not such a bad kitty, after all.

136

So I'm sorry you didn't like school very much, Kitty. But I want you to go home today understanding one thing . . .

137

Never!

CAN DOGS AND CATS EVER BECOME FRIENDS?

Dogs and cats can and will become friends, but they can't do this by themselves. They'll need your

MEOW?

help. The key is PATIENCE. Helping your pets to get along could take a long time and will require a lot of your attention.

First, take a few precautions. Trim the claws on your cat. Put the dog on a leash. Make sure the cat has a place to hide or escape if things get out of hand. And keep some treats on hand . . . you'll see why in a moment.

If you're bringing a cat into the home, keep her in her carrier and let the dog sniff the cat through the air holes. If the dog is calm, give him some treats as a reward. If he barks or is excitable, pull on the leash and tell him "NO" until he calms down.

ARF?

If you're bringing a dog into the home, also keep the dog in a cage if you can, at first. Bring the cat into the room by carrying her and petting her to let her know it's okay. If your cat gets wiggly or runs, don't punish her for being understandably anxious. Just pet her and console her.

Another tactic you might try is to keep both animals inside their respective carriers and place them

both in the same room with their doors facing each other. You should stay in the room, too, if only to give them both treats when they are calm. If either of your pets continues to be anxious about the

situation, you should be prepared to keep them separate from each other the best you can and repeat this process each day for as long as it takes.

In time, you should be able to train each pet to think of the other as another member of the family . . . an annoying member, perhaps, but part of the family nonetheless.

SIGH—I already have a lot of annoying members of my family.

•EPILOGUE•

Well, Kitty, I'm pretty disappointed with you that you didn't graduate. I can't help but think that maybe you just didn't try hard enough.

SIGH And I guess this means that you're the same old, cranky, ornery, disagreeable Kitty you've always been.

Your teacher Miss Dee kept telling me how much she likes you and how much she hopes that you'll be able to go back to school for another chance. She seemed to really like you, Kitty. But I don't know. I just don't see any reason to send you back to that school . . .

unless we really, really, REALLY have to.

I think I need more muscles.

You have enough. Now hush!

What does "subterranean" mean?

Go Fish!

GOFISH

NICK BRUEL

What did you want to be when you grew up?
I tell this story all the time when I visit schools. When I was in first grade, there was nothing I liked to do more than to write stories and make little drawings to go with them. I thought the best job in the world was the one held by those people who had the comic strips in the newspapers. What better job is there than to wake up each morning and spend the day writing little stories and making little drawings to go along with them? So that's what I did. I wrote stories and I drew pictures to go along with them. And I still do that to this day.

When did you realize you wanted to be a writer?
I always liked to write stories. But it wasn't until high school when I spent a lot of time during summer vacations writing plays for my own amusement that I began to think this was something I could do as a career.

What's your first childhood memory?
Sitting in my high chair, feeling outraged that my parents were eating steak and green beans while all I had was a bowl of indescribable mush.

What's your most embarrassing childhood memory?
Crying my eyes out while curled up in my cubbyhole in first grade for reasons I can't remember. I didn't come back out until my mother came in to pick me up from school.

What's your favorite childhood memory?
Waking up early on Christmas morning to see what Santa brought me.

As a young person, who did you look up to most?
My father. He was a kind man with a great sense of humor.

What was your worst subject in school?
True story: In eighth grade, I was on the second string of the B-team of middle school baseball. I was up at bat only twice the entire season. I struck out and was beaned. It was generally recognized that I was the worst player on the team. And since our team lost every single game it played that year, it was decided that I was probably the worst baseball player in all of New York State in 1978.

What was your best subject in school?
Art, with English coming in a close second.

What was your first job?
I spent most of the summer after my junior year in college as an arts-and-crafts director at a camp for kids with visual disabilities in Central Florida. I won't say any more, because I'm likely to write a book about it someday.

How did you celebrate publishing your first book?
I honestly don't remember. A lot was happening at that time. When *Boing* came out, I was also preparing to get married. Plus, I was hard at work on *Bad Kitty*.

Where do you write your books?

As I write this, I'm the father of a one-year-old baby. Because of all the attention she needs, I've developed a recent habit, when the babysitter comes by to watch Isabel, of collecting all of my work together and bringing it to a nice little Chinese restaurant across the street called A Taste of China. They know me pretty well, and let me sit at one of their tables for hours while I nibble on a lunch special.

Where do you find inspiration for your writing?

Other books. The only true axiom to creative expression is that to be productive at what you do, you have to pay attention to what everyone else is doing. I think this is true for writing, for painting, for playing music, for anything that requires any sort of creative output. To put it more simply for my situation . . . if you want to write books, you have to read as many books as you can.

Which of your characters is most like you?

In *Happy Birthday, Bad Kitty*, I introduce a character named Strange Kitty. I can say without any hesitation that Strange Kitty is me as a child. I was definitely the cat who would go to a birthday party and spend the entire time sitting in the corner reading comic books rather than participating in all of the pussycat games.

When you finish a book, who reads it first?

My wife, Carina. Even if I'm on a tight deadline, she'll see it first before I send it to my editor, Neal Porter. Carina has a fine sense of taste for the work I do. I greatly respect her opinion even when she's a little more honest than I'd like her to be.

Are you a morning person or a night owl?
Both. I suspect that I need less sleep than most people. I'm usually the first one up to make breakfast. And I'm rarely in bed before 11:00 PM. Maybe this is why I'm exhausted all the time.

What's your idea of the best meal ever?
So long as it's Chinese food, I don't care. I just love eating it. If I had to pick a favorite dish, it would be Duck Chow Fun, which I can only find in a few seedy diners in Chinatown.

Which do you like better: cats or dogs?
Oh, I know everyone is going to expect me to say cats, but in all honesty, I love them both.

What do you value most in your friends?
Sense of humor and reliability.

Where do you go for peace and quiet?
I'm the father of a one-year-old. What is this "peez kwiet" thing you speak of?

What makes you laugh out loud?
The Marx Brothers. W. C. Fields. Buster Keaton. And my daughter.

What's your favorite song?
I don't think I have one favorite song, but "If You Want to Sing Out, Sing Out" by Cat Stevens comes to mind.

Who is your favorite fictional character?
The original Captain Marvel. He's the kind of superhero designed for kids who need superheroes. SHAZAM!

What are you most afraid of?
Scorpions. ACK! They're like the creepiest parts of spiders and crabs smashed together into one nasty-looking character. Whose idea was that?

What time of year do you like best?
Spring and summer.

What's your favorite TV show?
I have to give my propers to *The Simpsons,* of course. But I'm very partial to the British mystery series *Lovejoy.*

If you were stranded on a desert island, who would you want for company?
I'm going to defy the implications of that question and say no one. As much as I'm comfortable talking for hours with any number of people, I'm also one of those people who relishes solitude. I've never had any problem with being alone for long periods of time. . . . You get a lot more work done that way.

If you could travel in time, where would you go?
America in the 1920s. All of my favorite literature, movies, and music comes from that period. I would love to have witnessed or even participated in the artistic movements of that period in history.

What's the best advice you have ever received about writing?
I had a playwriting teacher in college named Bob Butman who gave me superb advice on the subject of writer's block—it's all about PRIDE. It's a complete myth to believe that you can't think about what you want to write next because your mind is a blank. In truth, when you feel

"blocked," it's because you DO have something in mind that you want to put to paper, but you don't feel it's good enough for what you're trying to accomplish. That's the pride part. The best thing, I find, is to put it down anyways and move on. Half the challenge of the writing process is the self-editing process.

What would you do if you ever stopped writing?
I would seriously consider becoming a teacher.

What do you like best about yourself?
I have nice hands. They've always served me well.

What is your worst habit?
Biting other people's toenails.

What do you consider to be your greatest accomplishment?
Adopting our spectacular daughter, Isabel. Actually managing to get my first book (*Boing*) published comes in second.

Where in the world do you feel most at home?
Home. I'm a homebody. I like to work at home. I like to cook at home. I like to grow my garden vegetables at home. I like being in new and different places, but I despise the process of getting there. So, because I'm not a big fan of traveling, I just like being at HOME. It's a quality about myself that runs closely with my love of solitude.

What do you wish you could do better?
I wish I was a better artist. I look at the fluidity of line and the luminous colors of paintings by such artists as Ted Lewin, Anik McGrory, Jerry Pinkney, and Arthur Rackham with complete awe.

Find out where Kitty comes from and how Kitty copes when she confronts her greatest foe yet—her creator, **Nick Bruel!**

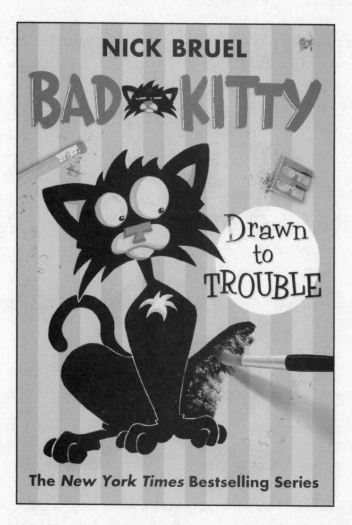

MEET THE CHARACTER

Okay. Let's get started!

We're lucky! We already have a character for our story. That's YOU, Kitty!

Yes, YOU! You are someone who has a personality, and as our story moves forward we're going to get to know you better.

In fact, Kitty, you're not just any character. You're going to be this story's PROTAGONIST, which is a fancy word that means you'll be the most important character in this story.

It's a bit like being the star in a movie.

Terry? Don't worry about him, Kitty. That was just a little FORESHADOWING, which is when a writer drops little hints about what's going to come later in the story.

But right now we need a SETTING, someplace where your story can take place.

Deciding on a setting is one great way to start a story.

For instance, maybe our story will be a great pirate adventure! In that case, we might set our story in the middle of the ocean!

Oops. Sorry about that, Kitty. Here . . .
let me help you up.

So ocean adventure was a bad idea. But don't worry, Kitty. We'll think of something. Maybe we could set our story in the jungle.

Sure! We'll make an exotic jungle tale set inside the wild, untamed forests of Africa with strange plants, mysterious noises, and huge, dangerous beasts of prey.